A Cat
Named
Egg

At the end of a street
on the edge of a town,
Was a rickety house
with no children around.

Outside of the house
the yard was in shambles,
Covered in weeds
and blackberry brambles.

The doors were all locked,
the curtains were drawn,
A homemade "Keep Out"
sign was stuck in
the lawn.

Inside was a woman with bows in her hair,
Rocking and rocking in her old rocking chair.

She had a cat on her lap and one at her feet,
There were two in the kitchen getting something to eat.

As a matter of fact there were cats all around,
Cats in the bathtub, cats curled on the ground.

Cats in the cupboards and cats on the bed,
If you were looking for something you'd find
a cat there instead.

Some people collect things like coconuts and hats,
But this lady had a collection of cats!

There was Reggie, Jaffy,
Beeswax and Peter,

There was Vincent
the magnificent marshmallow eater.

Ginger was wild-eyed
and scared of her tail,

Sandy was a gray cat that slept in a pail.

There was Simon, Alastair,
Alphie and Pat,

There was a cat named Slim
that was surprisingly fat.

There were cats that lived inside
and cats that stayed out,

There was a particularly feisty old cat she called Scout,

There was Mini,
Edward and
Mr. White,

There were two cats that liked to do nothing but fight.

Mandy and Joey liked to
cuddle together,

Oomp Oomp was crazy for a
string with a feather.

But the most peculiar cat of them all,
Was a cat that wasn't too big and wasn't too small.

If you walked in the house he was the first cat you'd see,
Smoking a pipe and watching TV.

He loved to play chess and was good at the game,
A strange cat indeed, and Egg was his name.

Egg? Yes, Egg. Like the one laid by a hen,
And packed in a carton with two more than ten.

Egg? Yes, Egg. It's that thing that tastes great,
Next to the bacon on your breakfast plate.

But how in the
world did he get
the name Egg?
From the shape of
his head? From a
mark on his leg?

Was it the way he looked
when he curled up in bed?
I asked Egg these questions
and here's what he said:

"A fine question indeed.
Thanks for asking, young chap."
Then he pointed his pipe at an
old dusty map.

"I was born on an island that was warm and quite pleasant,
When my parents passed on, I was raised by a pheasant.

But before I had even learned how to talk,
I was plucked from the nest by a hungry old hawk.

As we flew high above the wide open sea,
I squirmed and I squirmed until I wriggled free.

As I fell I looked down to see a ship fast approaching,

Then I splashed into a pot of eggs that were poaching.

The chef was quite shocked but he let out a laugh,

Then hired me on as part
of his staff.

He taught me how to separate
a yolk from a white,
He showed me the secret to
making frittata just right.

Unfortunately, the ship had trouble staying afloat,
But I managed to escape in an egg carton boat.

When I made it to shore I was starving and sick,
I needed a job and I needed it quick.

I was hired at a restaurant in the heart of the city,
And soon became known as the Quiche-Making Kitty.

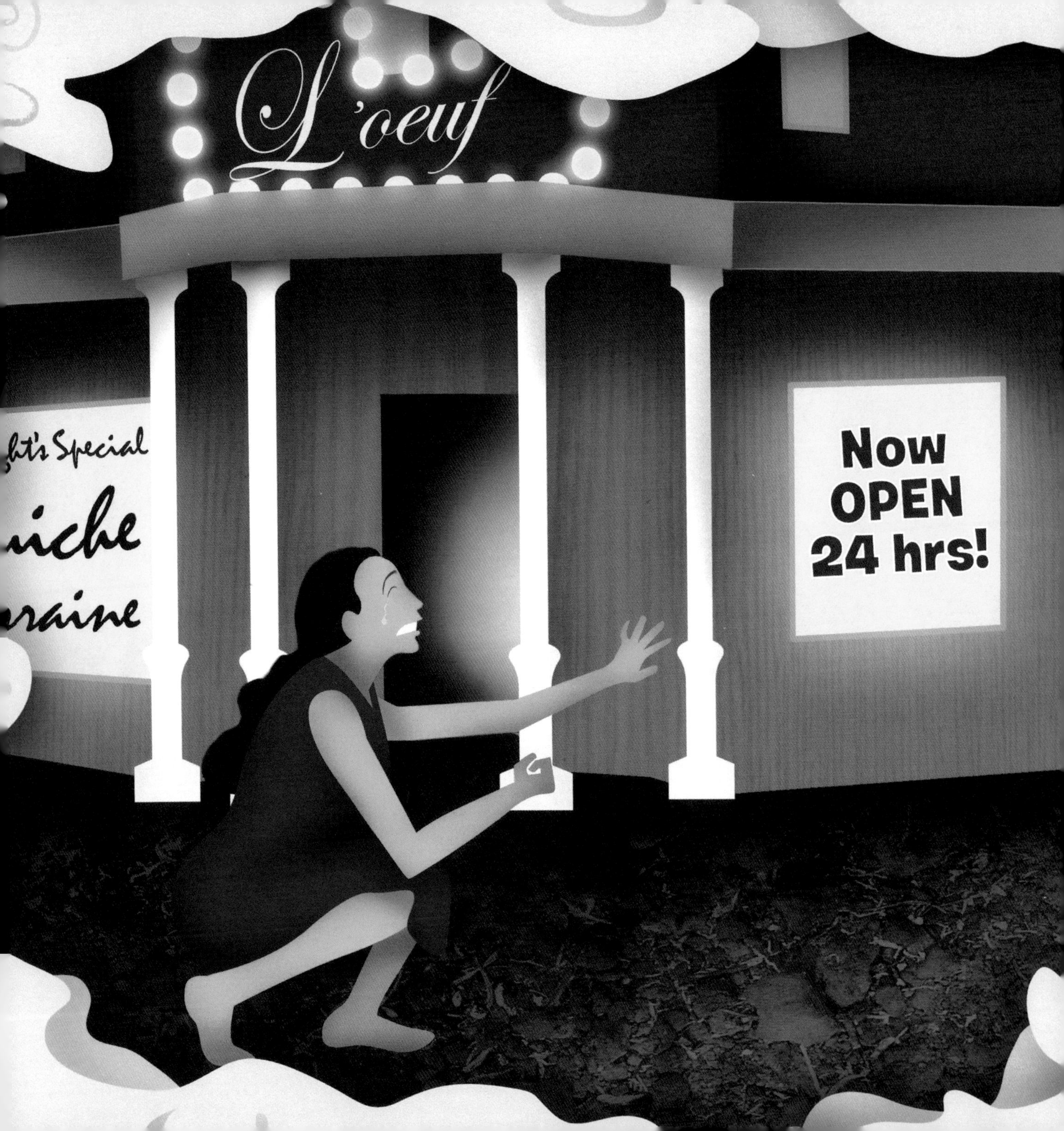
L'oeuf
Now
OPEN
24 hrs!

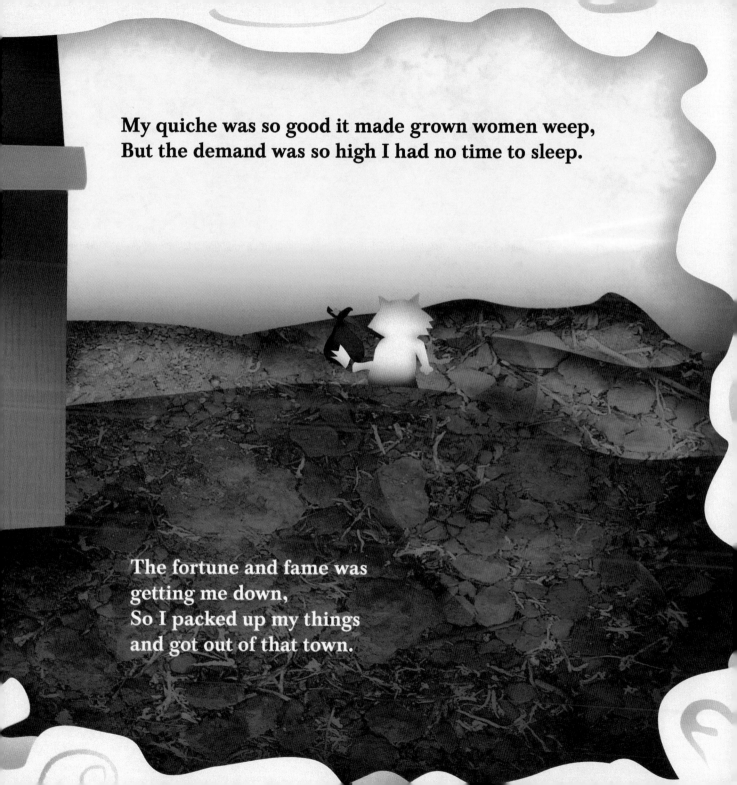

My quiche was so good it made grown women weep,
But the demand was so high I had no time to sleep.

The fortune and fame was
getting me down,
So I packed up my things
and got out of that town.

I spent a few years living in an old chicken coop,
Hanging out in bars, eating egg flower soup.

Then one day I woke up and just followed my feet,
And they led me to this house at the end of the street.

A nice old lady answered the door,
With a saucerful of eggnog she'd bought from the store.

As I lapped at the dish she suddenly proclaimed,

that
Edward
Gregory
Galoompus
would be my name

When I didn't object
she made it official,
And bought me a
tag engraved with
my initials.

And while my full name is something I fully support,
Most people just call me Egg for short.

So that's the story,
the whole kit and kaboodle,
Would you like to join us
for a bowl of egg noodles?"

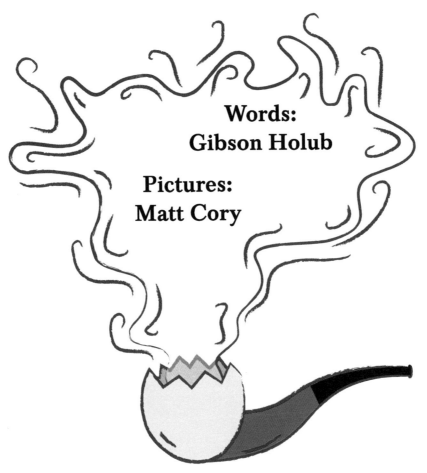

Words:
Gibson Holub

Pictures:
Matt Cory

Made in the USA
Lexington, KY
22 September 2011